The TRAVEL Game

by JOHN GRANDITS • Illustrated by R.W. ALLEY

CLARION BOOKS
Houghton Mifflin Harcourt
New York • Boston
2009

Clarion Books
an imprint of Houghton Mifflin Harcourt Publishing Company
215 Park Avenue South, New York, NY 10003
Text copyright © 2009 by John Grandits
Illustrations copyright © 2009 by R. W. Alley

The illustrations were executed in ink, watercolor, and acrylic.
The text was set in 17-point Electra.

www.clarionbooks.com

Printed in Singapore

Library of Congress Cataloging-in-Publication Data
Grandits, John.
The travel game / by John Grandits ; illustrated by R. W. Alley.
p. cm.
Summary: To avoid a nap, Tad plays his favorite quiet game with his aunt, and together
their imaginations take them from their home in Buffalo, New York, to Hong Kong.
ISBN: 978-0-618-56420-0
[1. Games—Fiction. 2. Imagination—Fiction. 3. Hong Kong (China)—Fiction.]
I. Alley, R. W. (Robert W.), ill. II. Title.
PZ7.G76584Tra 2009
[E]—dc22
2005017646

TWP 10 9 8 7 6 5 4 3 2 1

For my mother, Laurie,
and her sisters and brother
—J. G.

My family owns a tailor shop. It's on the first floor at 857 Broadway in the city of Buffalo, which you can find on the globe next to Lake Erie in the state of New York in the country of the U.S.A. on the continent of North America.

Grandpa and Uncle Myron make suits for men who can afford them—rich men. They also make suits for men who are hard to fit, which means they're extra tall or extra small or extra wide. When the circus comes to Buffalo, Grandpa and Uncle Myron are very busy.

Aunt Hattie makes pants shorter, waists larger, and shoulders narrower. Aunt Emily does fancy work. Grandpa calls her the Queen of Buttonholes. Mom takes care of the customers and watches the cash register.

And on Saturdays, I help out, too. I pick up the scraps of cloth that are all over the tables and the floor. I like that job. I carry the bolts of suit material to Grandpa and Uncle Myron. I *love* that job. I sweep up. I hate that job.

My grandparents, my parents, and I live in the apartments above the tailor shop. Dad doesn't work in the shop. He's a printer. Grandma doesn't work in the shop, either. She does the cooking for everyone. Lunch is the best meal. At 12:30 sharp, we close the shop and go upstairs to eat. This is what we're having today:

a *Wet pork chops.* They're very juicy, with lots of celery leaf.

b *Golumki.* Hamburger meat wrapped in cabbage. Left over from last night.

c *Applesauce.* I helped peel the apples.

d *Oven-cooked tomatoes.* Too yucky for me!

e *Fried mushrooms and onions.* Grandpa went mushroom hunting yesterday.

8

☐f *Homemade bread.*

☐g *Schmaltz.* That's pork fat with little pieces of bacon.
We use it instead of butter.

Grandma used to be a cook for the monsignor at St. Stanislaus
Church, so she's an expert.

9

After lunch, Grandma says,
"Tad, are you going to be a good
boy and take a nap today?"

That makes me really mad.
"I'm too old for a nap," I tell her.
"I don't take one on school days,
and I'm not taking one today.
I'm going back to work—like
everyone else."

Uncle Myron pats his tummy.
"I wish *I* could take a nap.
I ate too much."

"Of course you're going back to work, Tad,"
says Aunt Hattie. "But first, why don't we go to
your room and play the travel game?"

Now I have a very hard decision to make. Hattie
is my favorite aunt, and the travel game is the most
exciting game in the world.

Once when we played it, we went to India and rode on
elephants. Another time we explored the Great Pyramids
of Egypt. And another time, when we were on the Amazon
River in Brazil, we had to leap out of our dugout canoe
and swim through a school of deadly piranhas!

So I really, *really* want to play the travel game. But nearly every time we play, right before the end of the game, right before we get home from our adventure, right before it's time to go downstairs and get back to work . . . I fall asleep.

It makes me so mad! But today I have a plan. Every time I feel a little bit sleepy, I'll just think about those piranhas and that will pop my eyes wide open.

"Okay," I say. "First the travel game. Then work."

Grandma smiles.

Mom says, "Thank you, Hattie. You're a big help." She says it in Polish, but even though I don't speak Polish, I understand more than Mom thinks I do.

Aunt Hattie and I go to my bedroom. Here's what you need to play the travel game:

- *One globe*
- *The book* 1001 Pictures from Around the World *by George P. Smithers*

"Are you ready?" asks Aunt Hattie.

"I'm ready."

"Okay, you close your eyes, and I'll spin the globe. Then you put your finger down, and *that's* where we'll go." She says this every time. We've been playing this game since I was little, and I know how to play, but going over the rules is part of the game.

I close my eyes. I hear the spinning globe. I put my finger down. We look.

"Oh, no," says Aunt Hattie. "We're in the North Atlantic Ocean! We're on a raft, and there's no one around to rescue us."

I'm not worried. I know the rules. "We landed in the ocean. We can spin again."

"Right you are, boychik. Let's see where we go from here."

Aunt Hattie spins again. This time we have better luck. My finger is pointing to the bottom of China. "Oh, look!" she says. "We're right near Hong Kong. Have we ever been to Hong Kong?"

"No, we haven't," I say very seriously.

Actually, I've never been outside the city of Buffalo.

Now we go to the book *1001 Pictures from Around the World*. Aunt Hattie turns the pages. "Let's see . . . India, Malaysia, China . . . and here's Hong Kong. Look at this! There are four pictures."

We look at the first picture. It's wonderful! Hong Kong is nothing like Buffalo. Instead of streets, there's a lot of water. And instead of houses, there are lots of boats.

"Auntie, what's this? Why are there so many boats?"

Aunt Hattie adjusts her glasses and reads, "Aberdeen. The boat city of Hong Kong."

"What's a boat city? Where are the sidewalks? What are we going to do next?" I have a lot of questions.

"Well, let me tell you what happened, Tad. Remember when we were stuck on that raft in the Atlantic Ocean? Well, the *Titanic* came along and saved us."

Sometimes I think Aunt Hattie makes things up. "Are you sure, Auntie?" I ask. "Didn't the *Titanic* sink?"

"That was the *Titanic I*. This ship, the *Titanic II*, was heading for mysterious Hong Kong, and we went with it. And now we're right in the middle of a dock in the Aberdeen neighborhood."

"That's good, Auntie. We're safe."

"Yes, but now we have our first problem.
We don't have a boat."

"What do we do, Auntie?"

"We do what anybody does in a big city. We get a
taxi—only this is a *water* taxi."

I wave for the water taxi the way Mom does for a regular
taxi when we go to the big department stores downtown.

"That's good, Tad," says Aunt Hattie as we climb aboard. "But now we have our second problem. Everybody—I mean *everybody*—speaks Chinese. Do you speak Chinese, Tad?"

"No," I answer. "Do you?"

"No," says Aunt Hattie. "Polish and English. No Chinese. You'll have to act out where we want to go."

I love this part of the game.

The white pagoda owned by Aw Boon Haw, inventor the famous medicine Tiger Balm.
The streets of Hong Kong are so steep they have been terraced into hundreds of steps.

"Okay, the first place we want to go is here." Aunt Hattie shows me a picture of a round building with seven stories. The caption says, "The white pagoda owned by Aw Boon Haw, inventor of the famous medicine Tiger Balm."

Aunt Hattie opens her eyes wide. "Do you know what Tiger Balm is?" she asks. "It's medicine for sick tigers. When your tiger gets sick in Hong Kong, you take some Tiger Balm and rub it all over him. The tiger doesn't like the medicine. So first you have to chase him all over the room. Then you have to wrestle him to the ground. It's very dangerous."

"I don't know, Auntie. Isn't Tiger Balm for sore muscles? I think Dad has some in the medicine cabinet."

"Your father is very smart to be prepared," she says. "Anyway, now comes your job, Tad. You act out where we want to go for the water taxi man."

I get up and use my hands to show a round building with seven stories. Then I show how you give medicine to your tiger. I act out a very exciting and dangerous wrestling match. My stuffed tiger helps.

Then I say the name of the man who owns the pagoda, Aw Boon Haw, over and over, very slowly and clearly. And I say "Please," because it's good to be polite when you're in Hong Kong.

"I think he's got it, Tad," says Aunt Hattie. "Come sit beside me now, and we'll go see Hong Kong." Really, we're just sitting on my bed, but we cuddle together as if we're sharing the seat of a water taxi.

On the way to the pagoda, we pass the other things that are in *1001 Pictures from Around the World.* Aunt Hattie fills in the details. There are streets so steep that they have steps instead of sidewalks. And there's a big mountain right in the middle of the city.

It takes us a long time to get where we're going, and pretty soon it's dark. "At night, Hong Kong glows with beautiful neon lights," says Auntie.

We still haven't gotten to the pagoda, and Aunt Hattie starts
talking slower and slower. My eyes are beginning to close . . .
and I suddenly realize I'm falling asleep! So I start to think
about deadly piranhas jumping into the water taxi.

"Are there piranhas in Hong Kong, Auntie?" I ask.

But Aunt Hattie doesn't answer. She's snoring very softly.
I put my tiger under her arm and tuck them both in.

When I go downstairs to the shop, Uncle Myron says, "Where's Hattie?"

"She's in Hong Kong, taking my nap for me," I explain.

"Well, she'd better not stay too long. She's got three pairs of pants to shorten this afternoon," Uncle Myron says. "Anyway, now that you're here, go to the storeroom and get me a bolt of wool—the dark gray pinstripe."

I go to the storeroom and lift the roll of cloth onto my shoulder. I'm smiling because I'm hard at work with Uncle Myron. Grandpa is sitting cross-legged on his big table, stitching together a suit. Aunt Emily is making a complicated buttonhole for a lady's coat. Mom is at the front counter telling a customer that whatever it is she wants, it won't be ready until next week. And Aunt Hattie is napping upstairs with my stuffed tiger.

It's a lot of fun to travel the world, but it's nice to get back to work . . . and your family.

31

Author's Note

Aberdeen is a real village of boats moored in Aberdeen Bay on the southern coast of Hong Kong Island. In the past, many Aberdeen residents spent their entire lives on their boats, seldom coming ashore. They did their wash, cooked their meals, raised their children, and worked in various trades that supported their fishing. They even kept livestock on board—mostly different kinds of ducks and chickens but also goats! People still work and live there, and many Hong Kong residents keep small boats to go from place to place. But there are also water taxis.

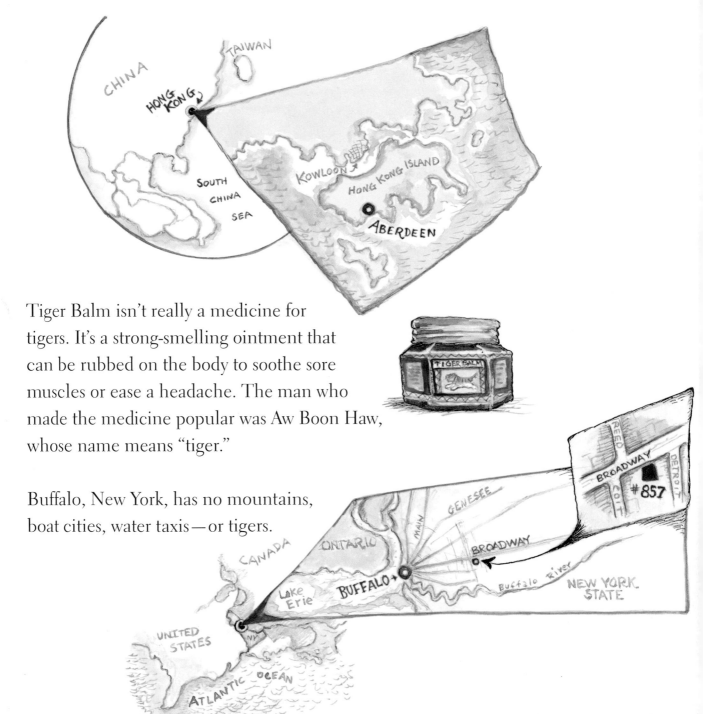

Tiger Balm isn't really a medicine for tigers. It's a strong-smelling ointment that can be rubbed on the body to soothe sore muscles or ease a headache. The man who made the medicine popular was Aw Boon Haw, whose name means "tiger."

Buffalo, New York, has no mountains, boat cities, water taxis—or tigers.